Christina Coghill
2001

For you
and your own special star

LITTLE TIGER PRESS
An imprint of Magi Publications
22 Manchester Street, London W1M 5PG
First published in Great Britain 1998
Originally published in Germany 1996 by
Baumhaus Verlag, Frankfurt
Text and illustrations © 1996 Klaus Baumgart
English text © 1997 Little Tiger Press

Printed in Singapore
ISBN 1 85430 480 1
5 7 9 10 8 6 4

Laura's Star

Klaus Baumgart

English text by Judy Waite

"I wish I had a friend," sighed Laura as she gazed out of her bedroom window. "Someone special, to share all my secrets with."
But there was no one listening – only the distant stars that winked and glittered like tiny jewels in the night sky.

Suddenly, something caught Laura's eye.
A streak of silver came whirling and twisting through
the darkness towards her. She gasped as it spun past her
window, so close she could almost touch it.
Something wonderful, something magical, was happening!
Laura quickly put on her dressing gown and slippers,
and hurried downstairs.

Outside on the shadowy pavement lay a little star,
fizzing sparks and colours like a giant sparkler.

"You're beautiful," Laura whispered, as she tiptoed
towards it.

A point of the star had broken, snapped off, when
it hit the ground.
"Don't worry," Laura told it, as she gently carried
it back indoors. "I'll soon make you better."
And up in her bedroom she managed to stick the
little star together again.

Later, Laura told the little star all her secrets, and it seemed to sparkle more brightly than ever. As if it were listening. As if it understood.

And, as Laura drifted off to sleep, she knew she'd found a special friend at last.

When Laura woke the next morning, the space on her
pillow was empty.
The little star was gone!
Laura was desperate. She searched under the quilt and
scrabbled through drawers and cupboards. She climbed
high to the top of the wardrobe and crawled low beneath
the bed. But it was no good. She couldn't find the little
star anywhere.

Laura felt cold and empty,
as if all the light had drained
out of her. Surely the
wonderful little star
hadn't been only
a dream?

When Laura came home from the playground,
Mum and Dad tried their best to cheer her up.
"How about your favourite jelly?" said Dad.
"Don't you like my funny hat?" asked Mum.
Laura couldn't answer, couldn't tell them why
she was so sad. Her star had gone for ever,
and she hadn't even said goodbye.

That night, as Laura climbed
wearily up to bed, she saw a strange
glow flickering from her room. Hardly
daring to hope, she pushed the door open.
The sudden blaze of light was dazzling. The little
star was back just where she'd left it, shining like a
thousand diamonds.
At first Laura could only stand and stare. Then, suddenly,
joyfully, she ran towards it.
"I know what happened!" she cried. "Stars only come out
at night. You must have been there all the time, and I just
couldn't see you. I should have known you wouldn't leave
me without saying goodbye."

Laura and the little star had a wonderful time.

They played games and did tricks, and Laura read it her
favourite book.
But Laura slowly noticed something. The little star began
to feel cold in her hand, as if it were fading away.

Laura stroked the little star gently with her fingertips as
it grew colder still. She felt the longing in it, and suddenly
she understood why her little star was dying.

Laura chose her four best balloons and carefully tied them
to the little star.
"Be safe," she whispered as she opened the window and
let go of the strings. "And be happy."
Slowly, the balloons drifted up into the darkness, and the
little star twinkled at Laura as it grew smaller and smaller,
until at last it joined the other stars in the midnight sky.

Laura didn't feel sad any more, for her star was back where it belonged. Each night when she went to bed, she could whisper her secrets into the darkness, knowing that the little star was somewhere out there, listening.